Guava Girl

PRAISE FOR *STORYSHARES*

"One of the brightest innovators and game-changers in the education industry."
– Forbes

"Your success in applying research-validated practices to promote literacy serves as a valuable model for other organizations seeking to create evidence-based literacy programs."

- Library of Congress

"We need powerful social and educational innovation, and Storyshares is breaking new ground. The organization addresses critical problems facing our students and teachers. I am excited about the strategies it brings to the collective work of making sure every student has an equal chance in life."
– Teach For America

"Around the world, this is one of the up-and-coming trailblazers changing the landscape of literacy and education."
- International Literacy Association

"It's the perfect idea. There's really nothing like this. I mean wow, this will be a wonderful experience for young people."   - Andrea Davis Pinkney, Executive Director, Scholastic

"Reading for meaning opens opportunities for a lifetime of learning. Providing emerging readers with engaging texts that are designed to offer both challenges and support for each individual will improve their lives for years to come. Storyshares is a wonderful start."
- David Rose, Co-founder of CAST & UDL

Guava Girl

Lorena Santana

STORYSHARES

Story Share, Inc.
New York. Boston. Philadelphia

Published in the United States by Story Share, Inc.

Storyshares
Story Share, Inc.
24 N. Bryn Mawr Avenue #340
Bryn Mawr, PA 19010-3304
www.storyshares.org

Inspiring reading with a new kind of book.

Interest Level: Middle School
Grade Level Equivalent: 4.6

9798885979627

Book design by Storyshares

Printed in the United States of America

Storyshares Presents

1

The report Talia had done on her summer reading book, "How the Garcia Girls Lost Their Accents," was due today, and the worst part was that she needed to give an oral presentation. She hated anything to do with public speaking and avoided it at all costs. But there was no way of getting out of this one. All her mental health days had been used up.

On mental health days, Talia's mom allowed her to stay home from school and do whatever she wanted, just because. Her mom believed that everyone, children and adults, should be able to take days off once in awhile without having to lie and say they are "sick." She thought that lying could actually manifest into reality. So, pretending to be sick to miss a day of school may lead to actual sickness.

"No," her mom would say. "If you're going to miss school, call it a well day and do something that you normally wouldn't do on a school day. Go to the beach or have a movie marathon."

Unfortunately, Talia's once-a-month quota had already been met.

Talia's mom was a kind woman who was far from the mainstream. In fact, Talia's whole family was kind of different, and people often commented on their blend of nationalities. Her father was from New Zealand, and her mother was from Mexico.

For the most part, growing up in an unconventional family was great. Most of Talia's friends thought it was cool that she didn't have a television or a microwave and that she lived in the oldest house on the block. While other families used heaters to warm up their homes in the winter, Talia's family would heat up the house with their fireplace. Even the light switches were unique. They were old push buttons made from mother-of-pearl.

Her mom had chosen the house but her Dad also had his own quirkiness. For example, he would come home from work and immediately change into a sarong. A sarong is like a skirt, It's a square piece of fabric that wraps around the waist. After changing, he'd make himself a cup of hot black tea.

He also had an accent that everyone loved and would use terms like "bush," in place of "outback." Instead of saying "bathing suit" he'd say "costume."

Lately, Talia had been growing a bit self-conscious about these differences. Why couldn't they have a TV, live in a modern house, and drink soda? Why couldn't she blend in, just a bit more?

2

Talia sat up and glanced around her bedroom walls. They were covered in artwork. Most of it was hers, except for the picture her dad had sketched of her when she was at a beach in New Zealand visiting his family. That had been a really great summer vacation. Her ukelele also hung on the wall, along with a poem that her mom had written to her in Spanish. It was a Haiku about her:

Talia

Flor divina que,

Salpica, abriedo con

Roco celestial

Oh, divine blossom,

Sprinkle and open the world,

With heavenly dew

Talia's mom was a writer. She'd tell stories to anyone who'd listen and she was good. One time...

Beep. Beep. Beep. The sound of her alarm put an abrupt end to Talia's reminiscing.

She got out of bed and put on her favorite Star Wars t-shirt, a jean skirt, and her favorite boots. She'd never worn boots with a skirt before, but today was going to be special. She checked herself out in the mirror and liked what she saw.

After breakfast, she went outside to gather guavas. She needed the guavas because at the end of her report, everyone would be given one. Talia loved guavas and was an expert on anything having to do with them. There were pink guavas, yellow guavas, and red guavas. All sorts of amazing things could be made from them, from jam, to smoothies, and even medicinal tea. That's why she had chosen to call her report *The Symbolism of Guavas in How the Garca Girls Lost Their Accents.*

Guavas were strewn all over the garden floor. Talia had to be careful because if she stepped on one, she could slip. She placed the guavas delicately into a bag. If they got bruised, their fragrance would become too strong.

Then she grabbed her backpack, said goodbye to her mom, and began walking to school.

It wasn't a long walk, but she had to be extra careful with her belongings. Lisa, her best friend, met her in front of their school. While they sat on a stoop waiting for the bell to ring, they shared a guava.

"I'm so nervous, Lisa," Talia told her.

"Why?"

"Because I hate it when everyone's watching me."

Lisa frowned, "Yeah, that's uncomfortable. It's going to be fine though, and over before you know it."

3

The bell rang and the girls made their way to English class. The sound of chattering students filled the room. Talia felt an oncoming wave of anxiety. Her stomach knotted up, swallowing became difficult, and her palms turned sweaty. She tried to take a deep breath, but her heart would not stop pounding.

Boom boom. Boom boom. Boom boom.

"Talia. Talia." Talia looked up at Mrs. Cohen. "Talia, you're up first. Are you ready?"

"Yes, Mrs. Cohen."

She stood up and made her way to the front of the classroom. Everything was moving in slow motion. Her feet felt heavy. Every time she took a step it sounded like Godzilla. *Boom. Boom.* She made her way to the front of the classroom. She took a breath and swallowed. She looked out at her classmates, and saw him. Chris Wood.

Chris Wood was not your typical teenage boy. He was lean, mean, and a self-esteem destroying machine. He gave her a cold, hard stare.

She took a breath, but her voice cracked the moment she began talking. She cleared her throat and started over.

"Today my report will be on *How the Garcia Girls Lost Their Accents*. I'm going to discuss the symbolism of guavas in the book. Guavas represent a loss of identity. This is especially apparent in the main characters's happiness when she goes back to the Dominican Republic. She eats guavas there and explains how they were her one *antojo*, which means craving in English. Do any of you ever crave things?"

Maggie raised her hand.

"Maggie?"

"I crave skittles."

A few people giggled.

"Maggie, I don't really mean cravings for candy. I mean a craving for something that brings back memories. For example, my mom makes really good quesadillas with corn tortillas. I often crave corn tortillas because they remind me of Mexico and my mom."

Suzi raised her hand. She was a Korean exchange student. "I cra..." Suzi struggled to say the word.

"Crave?" said Talia.

"Yes, craaaaave..." said Suzi, "...Kimchi! Korean food!"

"Kimchi. Yes, exactly!"

Sam raised his hand. "My grandmother makes me breakfast whenever I visit her. I could go and see her in the evening and she'd still make me a big breakfast. Sometimes, I crave breakfast for lunch."

A few eyebrows went up.

Maggie responded, "Your grandma makes you breakfast for dinner? That's cool!"

Mrs. Cohen raised her hand.

"Mrs. Cohen?"

"My mom makes matzo ball soup that no one else can replicate. When I have a cold, I especially crave matzo ball soup."

Lisa raised her hand.

"Yes, Lisa?"

"I've never had a guava before." She said it with a very serious face.

Was she kidding?

"Well, I brought guavas for everyone to taste because we have a guava tree at my house. I'll be passing them out at the end of my report."

"Okay!" replied Lisa.

Talia's report seemed to go well. Afterward, she passed out guavas as promised. When she got to Chris Wood, he took two, quickly stashing one away so that Mrs. Cohen wouldn't see.

"Chris, I only brought enough for each student to have one."

"Too bad, Guava Girl. I want two. One for now and one for later." Under his breath, he muttered, "And your report stank." Then in a very loud voice, he said, "Nice boots, Talia. Yee-haw!"

A few people snickered. Talia was so embarrassed, she just wanted to hide.

* * *

Later in the day, during lunch, Talia was walking across the quad and felt something hit her. It was a guava. She didn't even bother turning around because she knew exactly who had thrown it.

The end of the day couldn't come soon enough. When she finally found herself back in her room, she took off her boots, vowing to never wear them to school again.

Guava Girl

4

For a while after that, things were pretty peaceful at school. Chris had nicknamed her "Guava Girl," but for the most part, he left her alone.

A few months passed before once again, Talia had to prepare a report on a tradition from her family's culture. She immediately knew what she wanted to talk about, but wasn't sure how her classmates would respong, because it involved placentas. She asked Mrs.

Cohen for her opinion after class one afternoon, and Mrs. Cohen encouraged her to go out of her comfort zone and take a risk. "This sounds like a beautiful tradition and a fantastic theme."

Talia's report would be about the Mori tree planting tradition. Her father was not only from New Zealand, but was part Mori, and had taken part in this tradition when Talia had been born.

Unlike last time, she felt a strange sense of confidence as the days led up to her presentation. Not only did she have Mrs. Cohen's encouragement, but her dad had been very supportive in helping to prepare her report. He'd explained the importance of honoring the Earth in Mori culture, and had sat with her for hours answering all of her questions.

When the day finally came, a wave of pride washed over her as she stood in front of her classmates. "The Mori are the indigenous people of New Zealand," she began, "and they have many beautiful traditions. One of those traditions is that when a baby is born, the baby's placenta is planted under a tree. For those of you who don't know, the placenta is an organ that connects the fetus to the uterine wall to feed a baby while it's in the womb."

She saw a few eyebrows go up around the room.

"The Mori believe that all life takes place within the womb of the world," Talia continued. "And so to honor that belief, they bury the *whenua* and the *pito,* or the placenta and the umbilical cord, of a newborn baby, in a significant place. This practice still goes on today and reinforces the relationship between the newborn baby and the land of their birth."

Although some of her classmates seemed surprised by her report, overall, she felt it went beautifully. At the end, all of her classmates even clapped. All of them except Chris Wood.

5

Talia once again passed out guavas at the end of her report. When the bell rang, the classroom emptied. As Talia was packing up her materials, Mrs. Cohen commented on how much she'd loved Talia's report.

"Thank you, Mrs. Cohen." She felt as if she skated from the class, until she found Chris Wood standing outside, waiting for her.

"Placentas? Who does a report on placentas? I mean that's... really gross. In fact, it may be the most disgusting thing I've ever heard." He held a guava up to her. "And Guava Girl, these are nasty."

At that moment, Mrs. Cohen stepped out of the classroom. Chris Wood saw Mrs. Cohen and pretended to be charming. "I love these, Talia." He took a bite. "Will you bring some more soon?"

"I'm so happy that you like them, Chris," said Mrs. Cohen. "I agree, they are so good."

"Yeah, they are." Chris smiled even though he struggled to swallow.

Talia felt a sudden surge of courage and pulled a guava out of her bag, and handed it to Chris. She smirked. "Here's an extra one for you. I was saving it, but since you like them so much, you can have this one too!"

"Thank you... Talia." he muttered.

Mrs. Cohen smiled. "Well, I'm off to a staff meeting, but I'll see you two tomorrow," she said.

Before Chris could get another word in, she looked at him and said, "Guess what, Chris? Those guavas that you ate? They grew in my backyard. It's where my parents chose to bury *my* placenta when I was born."

* * *

After that day, Chris Wood stopped teasing Talia. And as she got older, her presentations just got better and better.

About The Author

Lorena Santana is a contributing author to the Storyshares library.

About The Publisher

Story Shares is a nonprofit focused on supporting the millions of teens and adults who struggle with reading by creating a new shelf in the library specifically for them. The ever-growing collection features content that is compelling and culturally relevant for teens and adults, yet still readable at a range of lower reading levels.

Story Shares generates content by engaging deeply with writers, bringing together a community to create this new kind of book. With more intriguing and approachable stories to choose from, the teens and adults who have fallen behind are improving their skills and beginning to discover the joy of reading. For more information, visit storyshares.org.

Easy to Read. Hard to Put Down.

www.ingramcontent.com/pod-product-compliance
Lightning Source LLC
Chambersburg PA
CBHW071230170626
46809CB00005BA/2015